MARGRET AND H. A. REY'S

Where Is Curious George?

A LOOK-AND-FIND BOOK

AROUND THE TOWN

WRITTEN BY CYNTHIA PLATT
ILLUSTRATIONS IN THE STYLE OF H. A. REY BY GREG PAPROCKI

HOUGHTON MIFFLIN HARCOURT
BOSTON   NEW YORK

Day is fine, George feels good!

He goes out in the neighborhood.

At the playground—what a view!

George is curious. What will he do?

Kids slide down, swing up high.

Kites are soaring in the sky!

Find a stroller, find a doll,

Sandbox shovel, soccer ball.

Bird nest nestled in a tree.

Now, that monkey—where is he?

Where is George?

In the school room, much to do.
Reading, math, and science, too!
Time to learn and have some fun
Till the bell rings and we're done.

Free time, fun time—
come here quick!
George is curious:
What will he pick?

Find a puzzle, letter blocks,
Beanbag chair, big red clock.
Pack of crayons, sharp and new.
My oh my, George, where are you?

Where is George?

Shiny engines, big black boots,

Firefighters down the chutes.

Ladder and hose are tucked away

Until it's time to save the day.

Alarm is ready to go *ding!*

George is curious: Will it ring?

Find a helmet, find two pots,

Find a dog with lots of spots.

A calendar to track the year.

Has that monkey disappeared?

Where is George?

Music plays, friends all meet.

It's like a store out on the street.

Farmer's market, crowd is hopping.

Apples, peaches—veggie shopping!

Tasty tidbits here to try.

George is curious.

What will he buy?

Find a pumpkin, loaf of bread,

Balloon escaping overhead.

Flowers tied up with a bow.

Wait, where did that monkey go?

Where is George?

Toys in every single space—
This is George's kind of place!
Toys for girls, toys for boys,
Children playing—happy noise!

Eyepatch for a pirate quest—
Is there treasure in this chest?

Find a red train, find a doll,
Funny clown, bright beach ball.
Twirling, whirling, spinning top.
Is George still inside this shop?

Where is George?

George is stopping at the zoo.
Monkey see, monkey do!
Run around, have some fun—
Visit animals one by one.

Stopping by to see the bear,
George is curious—what's in here?

Find a zoo map, find a pail.
Cotton candy, peacock's tail!
Sloth that's moving very slow—
Where'd that curious monkey go?

Where is George?

Sit right down. Napkin, please!

Here's a treat to make you freeze.

Read the menu, think it through—

The waiter will be right with you!

Many flavors . . . what to do?

George is curious—aren't you, too?

Find a blue hat, thick milk shake,

Giant spoon, ice cream cake.

Cherry on a huge sundae—

Come on, George—it's time to pay!

Where is George?

Cats and dogs, birds and mice . . .
Many pets—oh, how nice!
People taking such good care
Of the animals living here.

Folks all looking for a pal.
George peeks into this corral.

Find a rabbit, find a poodle,
Find a dog long like a noodle!
Parrot looking for a home.
Now where did that monkey roam?

Where is George?

Swing inside, take a look!

Stick your nose inside a book.

Story hour, time to play—

Open nine to five each day!

Helpers finding what you need.

George is curious: What to read?

Find a princess, find a dragon,

Giant penguin, book-filled wagon,

Dress-up clothes to make believe.

Did that monkey really leave?

Where is George?

Hit the ball, take a run,

Round the bases—so much fun!

Fans are clapping. Give a cheer.

Come and help out with the gear.

Big home run—happy roar!

George is curious:

What's the score?

Find a hot dog, find a mitt,

Big black dog, first-aid kit.

Trophy shining gold and bright.

Has that monkey taken flight?

Where is George?

Get your popcorn, get a drink,
Get some candy—shiny, pink!
Soon the movie will begin.
Folks are waiting with a grin.

Dimming lights, music groovy.
George is curious:
What's the movie?

Find a spaceship, three blue stars.
Find an alien from Mars.
Exit sign that's lit up red.
Tell me: Has that monkey fled?

Where is George?

Home at last—time for bed!
George just wants to rest his head.
Snuggle with a bedtime book
In a cozy reading nook.

Moonlight shining in a beam,
George is curious:
What will he dream?

Find a puppet, find a car,
Red maracas, firefly jar.
Find a kit for solving clues.
Will that monkey take a snooze?

Where is George?